# THE EXILE

AN OUTLANDER GRAPHIC NOVEL

## Diana Gabaldon

Illustrated by Hoang Nguyen

DEL
REY

BALLANTINE BOOKS    *    NEW YORK

# TO DEL CONNELL, A TRUE GENT WITH A SENSE OF HUMOR.

Published in the United States by Del Rey, an imprint of The Random House Publishing Group, a division of Random House, Inc., New York.

DEL REY is a registered trademark and the Del Rey colophon is a trademark of Random House, Inc.

ISBN 978-0-345-50538-5

Illustrations by Hoang Nguyen

Lettering by Bill Tortolini

Printed in the United States of America on acid-free paper

www.delreybooks.com

2 4 6 8 9 7 5 3 1

First Edition

# HOW THIS BOOK CAME TO BE

My mother taught me to read at the age of three—in part by reading me Walt Disney Comics. I never stopped (and was consequently appalled when I ran into Dick and Jane in kindergarten. Flipped through *See Spot Run* and put it back, wondering—aloud—why anybody would want to read *that*? I was not a diplomatic child).

Twenty-odd years later, I read a rather sub-par Disney story, though, and spurred by the reckless notion that surely I could write better than *that*, I sent a medium-rude letter to the editor of said comic line, essentially saying, "Dear Sir—I've been reading your Walt Disney Comics for twenty-five years now, and they've been getting worse and worse. I don't *know* that I could do better myself, but I'd like to try."

Evidently age had taught me nothing about diplomacy, but I did have the luck to have written to Del Connell, a true gent with a sense of humor, who wrote back to me and said, "OK. Try."

So I did. Del didn't buy my first story, but he did something much more valuable: He told me what was wrong with it. He did buy my second story (my first fiction sale ever; I literally bounced off the walls when I got his letter with the contract), and I wrote scripts for Disney for several years: Uncle Scrooge, the Beagle Boys, Daisy and Donald, Big Bad Wolf and Three Little Pigs, even the occasional Mickey Mouse story (I always preferred the ducks; Mickey was too much the straight arrow to be a really interesting character).

Eventually, the comics program stopped buying new scripts (someone at headquarters, having suddenly realized that they had forty years of Carl Barks scripts in the files, thought to ask why they were paying for new stories instead of simply reprinting those?), Disney sold their comics license, and I moved on to other things. But once a lover of comic books...

And so, when (years later) I had a literary agent and novels to my name, I told said agent that IF the opportunity to write a graphic novel should ever come along, I would seize it with both hands. And thus when a production company contracted for a movie option of my novels, I insisted that we must include an exemption in the option contract, since comic books would normally be covered under the "merchandising" clause—so that IF someone happened to come along and offer me the chance to write a graphic novel...

Well, one month later, someone did. That was Betsy Mitchell, the wonderful editor of the book you're holding. "I don't want a straight adaptation of *Outlander*," she said to me. "I want a new Jamie and Claire story, set within the parameters of *Outlander*."

"Well, *that's* a cool challenge," I said, scratching my head. "What if...?" So the story you're holding here begins slightly before *Outlander,* and is essentially the story as told from the point of view of Jamie's godfather, Murtagh. If you've read *Outlander,* you'll recognize some of the major events, but you'll also see a completely new storyline woven through them—all the things Claire *didn't* see or know about—as well as getting Murtagh's unexpurgated opinions of the whole affair.

Through Betsy's auspices, I found Hoang Nguyen, the magnificent artist who drew the story from my script, and the wonderful team of production people who've made this book a visual marvel.

So you and I have a lot of people to thank for this: Betsy and Hoang, Catherine MacGregor and Catherine-Ann MacPhee (who supplied the Gaelic), Russell Galen (my literary agent), Del Connell—and my mother. I hope you enjoy reading it as much as I enjoyed writing it!

Yours truly,

*Diana Gabaldon*

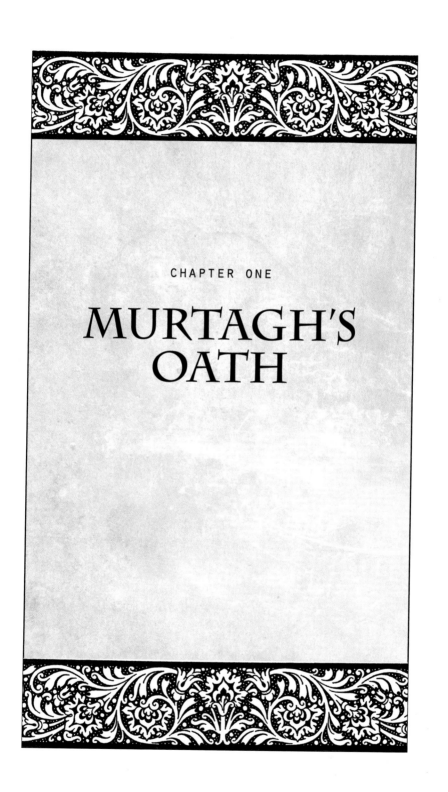

CHAPTER ONE

# MURTAGH'S OATH

Well, ye've
[b]en long enough
[a]bout it, lad!

Silkies!

OARK
OARK

*Outlander, specifically an English person

CHAPTER TWO

# TOO
# MANY FAERIES
# ALTOGETHER

I am, Madam, Captain Jonathan Wolverton Randall. At your service.

Oh? Well...I'll thank you to let me pass at once!

Not just at present, Chuck.* I'm asking myself...

*Slang for prostitute

...just why a whore abroad in her shift would be wearing her shoes? And quite fine ones, at that!

A *what*?!

‡MMMFF‡

Let—me—*go!*

Oh, I think not, Chuckie!

Get off! My husband will be looking for me!

Meanwhile...

Jesus H....

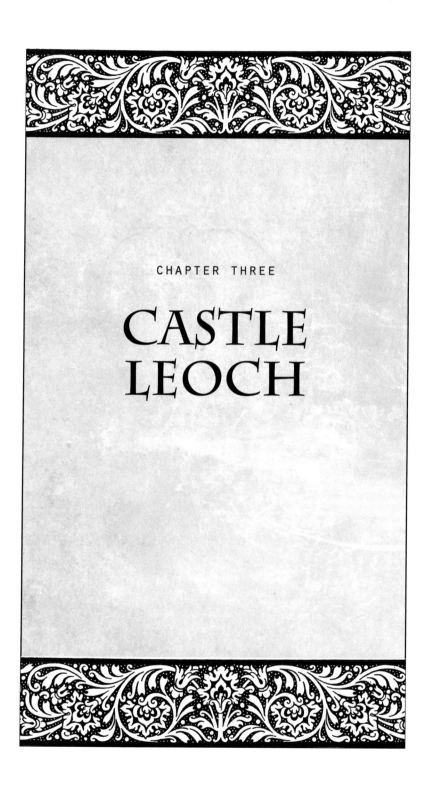

CHAPTER THREE

# CASTLE LEOCH

My sister—Jenny—she thought he'd kill me. So she—went wi' him.

God! Why did I not kill him the moment I saw him? Why would she not let me die, rather than...

And that...

That was later. At Fort William, where they took me. Obstruction, escape, and theft, they said.

You sound a right dangerous character!

Oh, I am that. A wonder ye think yourself safe in the same room wi' me!

t's true... in the 18th century!

Oh, God— Frank! Will I ever see him again!?

*my bro

CHAPTER FOUR

# HALL

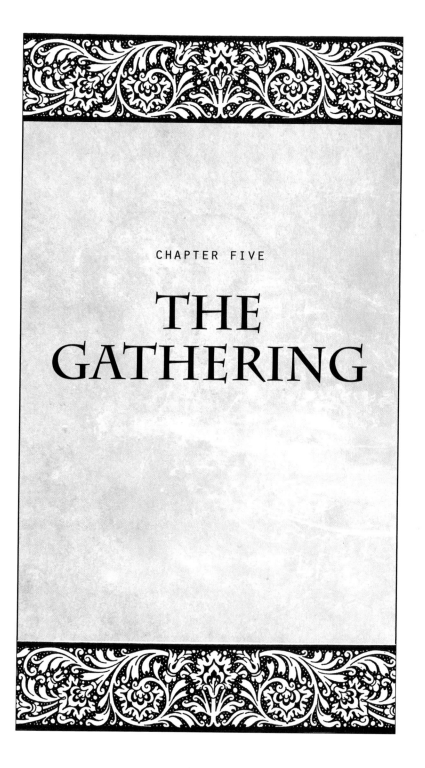

CHAPTER FIVE

# THE
# GATHERING

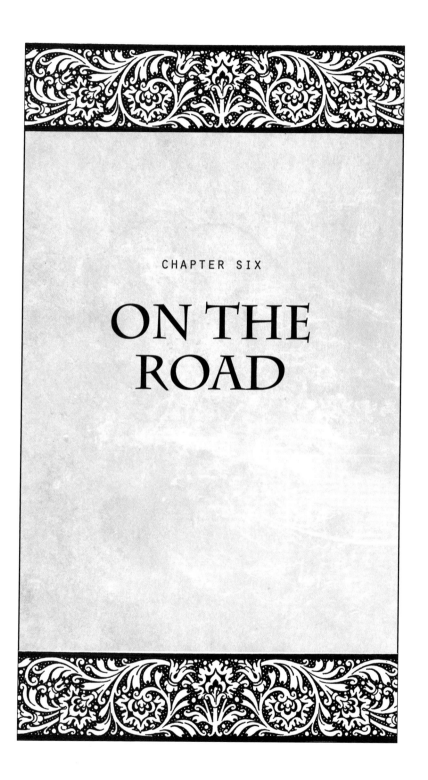

CHAPTER SIX

# ON THE
# ROAD

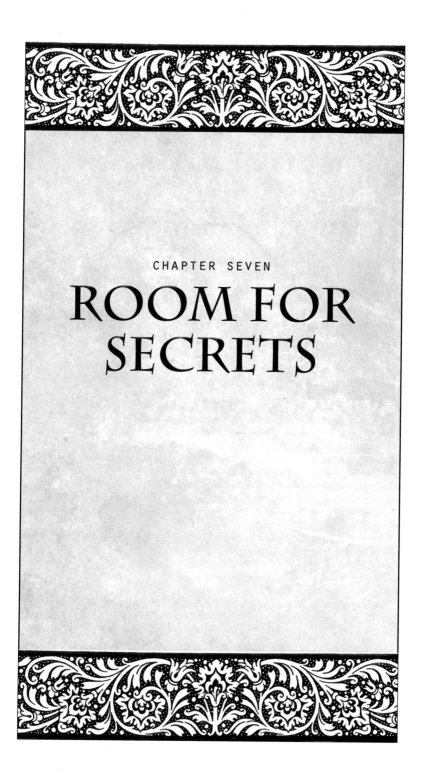

CHAPTER SEVEN

# ROOM FOR SECRETS

e've naught
espect between
w. And I think
ect has maybe
for secrets-
not for lies.

I'll ask
nothing that ye
canna give me.
But when ye do tell
me something, let
it be the truth.

I'll give ye
the same.

All right.
I'll give you
honesty.

Your
hands are so
warm.

Where did
you learn to kiss
like that?

I said I
was a virgin, not
a monk. If I find
I need guidance,
I'll ask.

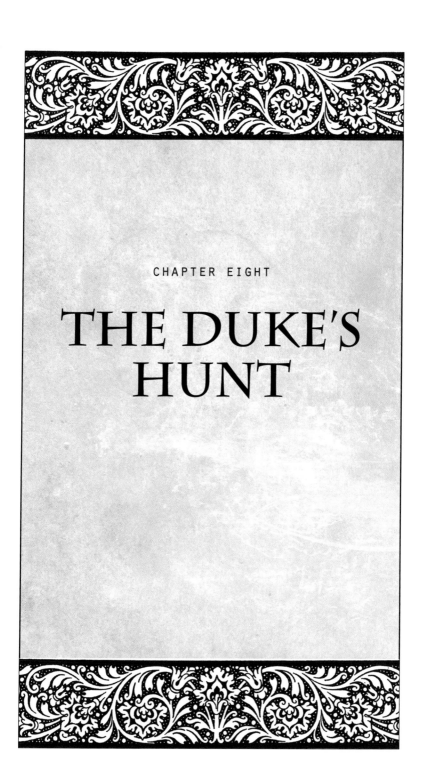

CHAPTER EIGHT

# THE DUKE'S HUNT

Jamie is not the only one who goes a-hunting with the Duke!

I'll find a gang of broken m[en] near the saint's p[...] in the Great Gle[n,] Geilie says. How t[he] devil does she k[now] these things?

Toward sunset that day...

I suppose she *would* know; she's a bloody witch, after all...

Gasp!

Stand and deliver!

Oh, I will! I've a proposition for ye, gentle-men!

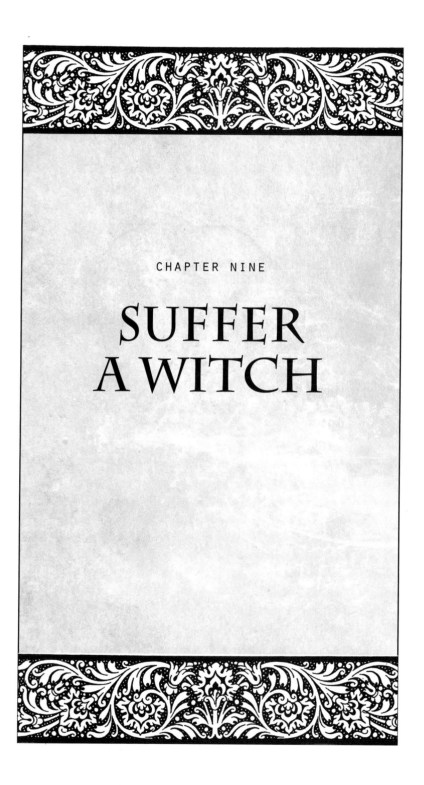

CHAPTER NINE

# SUFFER
# A WITCH

If this works—there's nay price on Jamie's head—there's nothing to stop him from going home to Lallybroch.

Aye, well... nothing save his own stubbornness. Perhaps I'll just club him o'er the head, tie him to his saddle, and...

What's the excitement?

# THE MAKING OF THE EXILE

A graphic novel is very much a collaborative work between author and artist, and the most important decision in the early creation of this project was selecting the art style that would best tell the story of *The Exile*. Diana Gabaldon deliberated over a number of art samples by possible artists. One was Hoang Nguyen, a California artist who was born in Vietnam and came to this country when he was nine years old. Nguyen's website, liquidbrush.com, overflowed with beautifully rendered female faces, many showing an influence from the popular Japanese manga style in which eyes are enlarged and faces delicate and elfin. But his talent was obvious—and when asked to supply additional samples, he provided a work in progress: a graphic novel set during World War I that showed his capabilities with male characters, action, and historical settings, all of which would be integral to bringing *The Exile*'s script to the sequential art form.

## CHARACTER DEVELOPMENT

Before he would be named the official artist, however, Hoang had to prove that he could bring to life the characters who have dwelled for so long in the author's imagination: Jamie Fraser and Claire Randall. His next task was to work up sample character designs based on Diana's descriptions.

### Jamie Fraser

*Diana's description:*

"A head taller than anyone else (he's 6'4", in a time when the average man stood 5'8"), wide-shouldered and muscular, but lean—built like a basketball player, not a football player or a superhero. A long, straight nose, faintly slanted dark-blue eyes, broad cheekbones, high brow, solid jaw with a wide mouth, usually turned up at one corner—thick, dark red hair (worn short but shaggy in opening, later in the story long enough to tie back), 'the color of a red deer's pelt.' He has a cowlick that lifts the hair off his brow (it's not standing on end; it just isn't hanging in his face). Young—he's 22—but well grown into himself, with a sense of strength and confidence. A smart-ass who knows he can back it up—but able to be gentle and thoughtful in private."

Diana gave this response to one early sketch.

*Notes in re Jamie—your second study of him has great presence and power, and isn't that far off. Of course, getting him just right is particularly tricky, because (as you saw in the first book) since it's written from Claire's viewpoint, she describes him minutely and repeatedly—which means all the readers (who've read all the books, often multiple times), have very detailed and fixed notions of him.*

BEFORE

*I did (out of curiosity) show the sketch to a group of fans who were hosting a private party for me at a recent conference, just to see how their impressions matched with my own. They all went, "Ooh!" but then said (basically), "He's too pretty." Mostly a function of the mouth, I think, though (trying to get as specific as possible in terms of features here) this drawing has too much chin and not quite enough nose. Also a little too thick and burly through the neck; he is a warrior, but we also need an impression of youth and some vulnerability. The most general comment that wasn't based on features was that they wished they could see him smiling. He is, as you'll have noticed, possessed of a marked sense of humor, and it generally shows on his face.*

AFTER

The Internet abounds with fan-created artistic renderings of the *Outlander* characters, and as it happened, two of Diana's readers supplied pieces that turned out to be extremely helpful in finalizing Jamie's appearance. One was this piece, described by Diana:

*The attached drawing was sent to me by a German fan. It's a very young Jamie, aged about 13 or 14, and by good fortune, it actually does look very much like him. This is definitely his nose and heavy eyebrows, and the facial bones and proportions are pretty close, too. He doesn't have a cleft in his chin, though.*

ART BY CHRISTINA SPIELBAUER, HTTP://79CHRISTINAS.DEVIANTART.COM

The second photo reference was created by a fan who touched up a photograph of model Gabriel Aubrey to give him red hair and the background of a Scottish loch. We don't have Aubrey's permission to use the resulting piece in our book, but at press date it could be found at this URL:

HTTP://SMG.PHOTOBUCKET.COM/ALBUMS/V514/AAG567/ ROLE%20PLAYING/?ACTION=VIEW&CURRENT=JAMIE12.JPG

Another...useful, shall we say...photo of Mr. Aubrey appeared on theinsider .com in their "Shirtless Celebrity of the Day" section. Says Diana:

*That sort of long, lean body in the "shirtless" pose is what Jamie looks like, though he's a good bit more "cut" than Mr. Aubrey, owing to an active life. <cough>*
*Now, if we can just find a good shot of Mr. Aubrey's naked behind...*

That final comment was part of a lengthy discussion among author, artist, and editor regarding just how Jamie should look in the nude scene on page 11. Suffice it to say that the version which appears in this book is the result of extensive research.

### Claire Beauchamp Randall

*Diana's description:*

"Tall for a woman—5'6", versus an average of 5'1"—with wildly curly light-brown hair. (About shoulder-length to begin, longer later in the story. Her hair has a personality of its own.) Dark brows and lashes, arresting whisky-colored eyes. Noticeably pale, translucent skin and a strong sexual presence (well-developed breasts and round bottom, though generally slender build). Oval face, well-defined cheekbones, and a lush but determined-looking mouth. Nose not remarkable. Definitely not a teenager; she's 27 here, and should look intelligent and competent—she's been a combat nurse during World War II. Major-league sense of humor, but not willing to be messed with."

Hoang's vision of Claire emerged quickly. Diana asked him to make her hair curlier, but she ended up essentially unchanged from this early sketch. Her figure came in for discussion at various points as the graphic novel proceeded. The original version of the scene in which Claire stumbles across Jamie in the stable during her aborted attempt to escape Castle Leoch presented her as quite voluptuous. As Diana wrote to Hoang:

*I second Betsy's motion regarding Claire's breasts on page 96 (panel 3). What my daughters refer to as "the boobage" might be getting a trifle out of hand on some of the later pages in this sequence, too; I think it's great for Claire to be buxom, but she's about twice as big in the bosom here as she was back on pages 34 and 35. Her figure in the early pages, right after she comes through the stones, is very good, I think.*

## CLOTHING AND ACCESSORIES

Scotland in the eighteenth century required visual research on dozens of topics, and Diana supplied numerous reference books for Hoang's use. She filled frequent emails with further information. Here is one of particular interest.

*The Scottish clans did wear kilts (and women's shawls, called arisaids) made in checkered-weave patterns called tartans, and it was known in the eighteenth century for families to have a specific pattern (or sett). But there was no such thing as a traditional clan sett. You would see groups of related men wearing similar colors and patterns, just because they were all getting their cloth from the same local weaver, and the weaver was using the dye-plants that grew nearby, and a limited number of variations on his (weavers were mostly men) usual pattern. But there was no custom of a clan all wearing a particular clan tartan. There's* not a lot of pictorial evidence from the Highlands, because only the very wealthy had their portraits painted—but there is one well-known painting of the two sons of the Duke of Argyll, wearing tartan. One boy is wearing a kilt, waistcoat, and jacket; his brother's wearing trews (tight-fitting trousers), a waistcoat, and jacket—and between them, they're wearing six different setts, even though all of them are done in the same colors.

Then along came the Rising under Bonnie Prince Charlie, and when the Scots were defeated at Culloden, the British government passed the Diskilting Act, which prohibited Highlanders from wearing tartan, owning weapons, or playing the bagpipes (which were considered a weapon of war). So no tartans at all were worn in the Highlands (at least officially) from 1746 to 1786, when the Act was repealed.

OK, along comes Queen Victoria and her husband—and Sir Walter Scott—and among the three of them, they romanticized the Highlands and made it fashionable to go to Scotland (which previously was considered a howling wilderness). And the Prince Consort took to wearing a kilt when he was in Scotland. Whereupon the Lowland woolen merchants (the Lowlands of Scotland are culturally distinct from the Highlands, being more or less English-speaking and not Gaelic) recognized a Good Thing, and swung into gear, producing "traditional" clan tartans. All of what most people think are traditional setts were in fact invented by these nineteenth-century woolen manufacturers.

The thing is, these merchants did such a good job of promotion (and people are so generally ignorant of history) that now everyone assumes that these tartans are in fact traditional, and that the Frasers, for instance, have always worn a scarlet, green, and black dress tartan and a blue and brown hunting tartan, while the MacKenzies wore dark green and white, etc. Whereas in fact, a lot of MacKenzies may have worn some variation of green and white—but not necessarily, and not all of them.

*The problem, of course, is that "everybody knows" that clansmen are supposed to wear distinctive tartans. It wasn't possible to stop the story (in* Outlander*) dead and explain all this about tartans (Claire wouldn't have known it, in any case) so I had to sort of walk the line between what I knew to be historically accurate, and this very popular misconception.*

*And that's probably way more than you wanted to know about tartans.*

## THE MATTER OF THE QUAICH

Having never seen a quaich, Hoang drew it the first time at almost the diameter of a dinner plate. Diana sent the attached photos and note.

*Attached are some photos of two quaichs I have—I've never seen one bigger than the larger one of these (and drinking one of these full of undiluted whisky would knock a normal person on their ass, believe me—assuming they could do it without strangling). I have very small hands, and you can see how the quaich fits me—I should really have made my husband hold it and taken the picture myself, but didn't think of that.*

# THE MATTER OF THE WEDDING-NIGHT SCENE

There was no drawing of the veil of night over Jamie and Claire's wedding bed. Hoang's original version of the scene on page 142 was quite revealing—so much so that this editor printed out the page in full color and carried it around to various departments of Random House to ask others whether it was too graphic, even for a "graphic novel." And although that version of the art brightened the day of many a hardworking publicist, editor, and marketing manager, it was decided to go with a slightly less revealing version. Diana acquiesced:

> *I like the original very much myself, though I think moving Claire's arm to obscure her nipple wouldn't ruin it. If we do need to tone it down, though, I'd vote for discreet blanket-draping, rather than tucking the legs out of sight— that doesn't seem realistic.*

Interested readers may access the original version on Diana's website at www.dianagabaldon.com.

# A FINAL WORD FROM DIANA

Those of you who've read the original *Outlander* novel (the record, I believe, is held by the woman who wrote to tell me she'd read it twenty-three times. I'm very flattered, of course, but I sort of hope she actually has a life, too....) may notice small variations of detail from the text. This was deliberate, and done either to accommodate the original dialogue in a constrained space, or for visually artistic reasons. For example, while in the original novel Claire arrives in 1743 wearing a dress sprigged with peonies, she's wearing a plain blue 1940s housedress here. The style of the dress is exactly what she would have been wearing, but using a solid color instead of a print makes the composition of the panels more striking. (For the same reason, tartan colors occasionally vary from their original description.)

A collaborative project ideally gives both artists scope for their individual talents, and it was a thrill to me when I could put a direction in the script like, "I need a half-page scene here where Angus Mhor beats the s— out of Jamie, but details not important. Go for it!" and see what Hoang's imagination and talent came up with. The results were always more than gratifying.

Do keep in mind, though, that what you're seeing here is really not a literal transcription of what's inside my head when I see these characters. They can't be, for one thing—collaboration has its limits, and those usually stop well short of telepathy—and for another, this is a graphic novel; characters are approximations appropriate to the form. Naturally, every reader brings his or her own background, expectations, and personal preferences to the visualization of fictional characters. All you have to do to realize this is to glance at some of the *Outlander* fan art available on the Web, which ranges from the sublime to the...er...well. <cough>

Just bear in mind that if you could see inside my head, almost all of you would exclaim, "That's not what I thought Jamie looked like!"

Anyway, I hope you've enjoyed this book, and its unique angle on the *Outlander* story. For those of you who haven't read the original novel... *The Exile* covers approximately the first third of *Outlander*. So if you want to find out what happens next, see the following page for a complete list of the books in the Outlander series.

*Le meas agus,**

*With respect and best wishes*

*Also by Diana Gabaldon*

# THE OUTLANDER SERIES

# THE COMPANION VOLUME

THE RANDOM HOUSE PUBLISHING GROUP
www.DianaGabaldon.com